People say "Lissa be YOU"... Sex is me and sex is art judge I don't give a fuck the Erotic Aphrodisiac will continue...

Lissa

I have a habit of when old things come back, I either pick up where it/we left off or make something completely new out of it. With me, sex is a way of letting your spirit(s) and soul communicate. Sex is art. I could think up a sex scene in my head and I could cum having never even touched myself. I've never masturbated. I'm addicted to sex.

As I'm laying down on this man couch, I'm thinking, "Bitch are you really here for sex therapy?" I'm also thinking, "Why do I always say the first thing that comes to my mouth?" Yes I said 'mouth' because if it came to my mind, I probably would word some shit different. Maybe, maybe not.

Mr. Jo asked me if I'd ever been addicted to anything else.

Mr. Jo was my third counselor at this point in my life. He was in his fucking 70s! Real cool dude; very blunt and ex-military.

I laughed at him and I said,"Yes I'm addicted to big dicks." I laughed because I know you're thinking, "what"?He asked, "What's the fucking difference?" This is what I loved about this man - he just said it how he felt. I answered him, "Sex can be a variety of many things but sometimes a big dick is just a big dick." Still confused by my answer, I chose to tell him two different stories.

The Big Dick Experience – Carin called me and said Boogie from the D wanted to link up. Mind you, I just came from a second go-round 'on-and-off' relationship with Tyler. Randomly messing with Vince toxic ass whenever I felt like it. Hell, not to mention, it was the summer after senior year - fuck it why not. We talked a little before but let's be real, we didn't know each other. I knew his real name, alias, his age, where he went to school and his apartment of course. He stayed on campus at MSU. I knew I shouldn't have went, but sex was a way to let go of some steam and stress (Yeah, I really think like a nigga). Again, I ignored all the signs of "Bitch this shit bout to be whack." I went anyways; I pulled up to the dorms or whatever, and my best friend was already outside waiting on me. This bitch just laughing. I asked"Ho what's funny?" She replied, "Girl, he been waiting on you. You been dodging him for Vince stupid black ass. Let that shit go he a ho and he fucked everybody in our class." I'm thinking she's really right. This nigga got a girl and we are not together. I really just fucked with him because he took my virginity, and I was shy. I had a banging body but I hated my body. I said nothing though, as I nervously walked through the door and into his room.

I sat there like I didn't know what I was there for, because I got turned off. 'A' came in there with his many teeth wanting to talk and Boogie was on the P3 (PlayStation 3). Carin was in there with the other many roommates so finally I asked,"Are we fucking?" He looked at me and said, "I want to make love to you." So many thoughts ran through my head; the most important one: "I'm about to fuck him and leave." To get things rolling, I stood up for him to undress me, and he did, while lightly planting kisses on me from head to toe...literally. Fool even kissed my eyes. I tried to relax and get into it, but he was so nervous. He started panting and I was just standing there. I thought, "Well, maybe he's a virgin." I wasn't experienced at sex but I was not acting like him. I got tired of whatever he was trying to make happened and just laid there. I was so not in the mood; I didn't even want my pussy ate. Finally, he pulled his dick out!! His skinny ass had a big thick dick. Immediately, I was turned back on. I have this thing for not laying on my back, so I jumped on his dick and for a minute, I just had to sit there. I had to figure out how to fuck his dick and how to fuck and not make too much noise. The whole minute I sat on his dick, he didn't move, make his dick jump, no nothing. I knew then, I would have to fuck him for me. As I'm riding his dick, I grabbed his shoulders because I wanted to lean in and feel more. I needed that pain. This motherfucker tried to kiss me; I leaned back and I told him to fuck me. He wanted to. He even tried, but he was nothing but a big dick and I felt like if I'm not satisfied,then motherfucker, you won't be enjoying it. I couldn't take anymore; I seriously got up. God and Carin must have heard my prayers, because big baby came knocking on the door.

"Girl come on in, ain't shit happen in here," I yelled, like she wasn't already halfway in the room. "Lis you crazy– ," I cut her off because I knew she heard it in my voice and if she would have said anything else, I would of snapped on him. I said, "Bitch walk me out. I got a headache and my stomach hurt." I was dead ass serious; he was in my guts and it was so horrible, I got a headache. As I'm walking out, 'A' ran back in the room where Boog was and he is snickering, and I heard this nigga say, "Damn my nigga, smell like some good sex in here." I immediately turned around and I don't know how many motherfuckers were in there but I stated, "Naw! It smells like some bullshit in here cause yo' homeboy can't fuck." I walked out and Carin was sitting there with her mouth open, because she was staying over there for the night. I wouldn't have even been mad if they sat up all night talking about how crazy of a bitch I am. I sat there for a minute because like I said, I ignored all the signs on the way there. Man, I left a light on and had to get a boost. I was on a time limit. I cracked my phone and lost 20 dollars. I said, "Yeah bitch, that's what you get." He texted me for a week after that. We communicated, but when he talked about messing around again, I had to let him know he was nothing but a big dick. He replied he had never had sex before. I did not feel bad because if you don't know what to do, let someone guide you. We both can't be that bad a sex.

As I sat there catching my breath.I looked over to see if Jo is still up. I know that was a lot to process, and this was our first sex therapy session. I came for anger management, too. Jo replied "Ms. Hunter, this is very different from our other sessions. You do know our sessions are recorded?" They're recorded because we've done hypnosis sessions as well with my fucked up ass. I started laughing and I said, "I'm going to need these recorded sessions when I write a book because no one is going to believe me. Todd is dead and I can't just share these stories with anyone. But anyways, this is where sex and just a big dick makes a difference."

Great Sex – Same year months apart.

Marqus called and told me that he was coming to town. "Let me catch you up on Marqus," I said. Marqus is a dude I met when I was 16 years old. First day we met, we laughed and chilled all day. He was kind of short, pretty brown eyes, beautiful hair (it was really just waves), tattoos and milk chocolate complexed depending on what angle you look at him. Marqus is very smart, great at basketball and could dance his ass off. I was excited when I knew he would be coming the weekend after his birthday. We never did anything besides kiss. He stayed in Denton so we kept it long distance and whoever he was with there he was with, and whomever I chose here, I had. I was single, but I fucked with Vince off-and-on since the first time we fucked. I knew I wanted to wait for him. I cut everybody off and I read my Zane books; to relax and get an idea of what I wanted to do to him when he came. I had about 3 months to plan shit out, making sure he arrived after my period (I didn't want anything to ruin that weekend). Well, I fucked up and fucked Vince like one more time. Everything about that night felt so fucking wrong. I did not feel bad because at that point in time I was single; he was a ho…shit my ho, no matter who he was with. I was waiting, but what if Marqus never showed?

All the details aren't important at the moment. However sure enough, 3 weeks later, Marqus called and told me he was in Wichita. It was Friday night. No kids and no bills. The only worries I had was what I was going to wear. The night approached and the hottest spot was club Chameleon. Crazy how life works: I met Marqus through my older sister's baby daddy. They played basketball together, but when he came to visit, he stayed with my sister's fiancé - which is his cousin. Their moms are sisters. Anyways, we went out. I wore a yellow half-jacket with some high-waist pants and these neon colorful heels (my ex had got me) with a gold necklace and bangles – not too much; I needed everything to come off with ease.

Let's skip the club scene. We went back to the apartment and we were fucked up. Everything that happened, I wanted to happen. My sister and her fiancé went in the room and I was so drunk, we didn't leave the living room. Drunk off 'Adios Muthafuckas,' I kissed him. He kissed me back, but he didn't stop. In the dark, I closed my eyes. He unzipped my jacket and told me to relax. As he's pulling down my pants, he's kissing and licking me down. It was nothing like I was used to. He took his time. He said, "Open up, I wanna taste you." I was already dripping from the thoughts of fucking this man; I believe I came before he even touched me. He stuck one finger in his mouth, and stuck it inside of me and then licked it off. I closed my eyes again because my eyes had adjusted to the dark and I could see him (as if slurping my juices off his fingers wasn't enough already). I spread my legs open and he put his face in, catching the warm fresh juices rolling down my pussy before they got to my ass. He sucked out the cream. I wanted his dick because anymore kisses like that and we would of went through the floor and the second floor would have been no more. He put on that condom and rammed his dick inside of me real hard one time, then he made love to me... sweetest thing I've ever felt. He had an alright-size dick; it was big but average. There was not one part of me that went untouched. This was the dude I dreamed of. The dude I should have lost my virginity to. I waited two years for all of this, and it was worth whatever we went through to get to that point. That night, I had an out-of-body experience; I came back to back. I started shaking so bad, I had to look up what had happened when I was going in and out of life. That night, he whispered he loved me and while we kissed, I squirted on his dick. I was super embarrassed. I'm feeling like I pissed everywhere and he's loving it. It turned him on more. I don't know how many times we stopped or slowed down, and I enjoyed every minute. Finally, he busted and fell in me. We laid there for a minute, stuck like dogs. He took his condom off. I passed out and woke up to him drinking my juices. It's nothing like mama's nectar. He didn't have to tell me, I knew already. We fucked once more and held each other like 2012 was near. (They said the world was ending)

The next morning, I woke up feeling weird. I didn't know if I was still drunk, or was the sex so good, I was slightly sick to my stomach the morning after. I got up and rushed home. I showered and I noticed I was bleeding, but it wasn't my period. It was a different type of blood. My sister started blowing me up. Oh yeah, I took her car. I told her I was headed back and by the time I got back, everybody was up. Marqus ole' goofy ass told the whole house we fucked. I was sick to my stomach and denied it all - I didn't care at that point. I got tired of my sister and brother-in-law asking that I said, "No, but we can fuck right now." In between me leaving and coming back, somebody went in the trash and found the condom. "Oh, so yall nasty and private investigators? Oh ok, so how ya'll don't know he didn't leave and fuck somebody while we was sleep," I exclaimed with a straight face. He was outside talking to his bitch so what could he say? I lied so good that by the time he got off the phone and came inside, everybody was ready to jump on him for lying. But he didn't lie, I was just disappointed he told our business like that. He was in town for another day, but I had to figure out what was wrong with me. For the rest of the day, we texted and I explained to him everything I was experiencing.

For the first time ever, Jo cut me off and said, "Just what in the hell happened next?" losing all professionalism. We both laughed and I told him that would be another session. I wanted to let him in, but in order for me to do that, he had to first force his way in. He wanted to know when the addiction started. What happened in my childhood that made me want to take on sex as a challenge? Totally ignoring the childhood comment, I explained to him I was addicted to sex before I even had sex......

Losing It

12 years ago today, I lost my virginity. Valentine's Day – what better way, right? Well, that's what you would think – hell, that's what I thought. I didn't plan on losing my virginity that day, it just sort of just happened. Vince and I had been dating a few months. We said our "I love you's" and had gone through plenty of break ups, but we were on today, and I was super excited to see him at school. As I'm walking out the door for school, he texted me and told me he wasn't feeling good and was going to stay home.

Well… there went my morning. I didn't give a fuck about him being sick – hell his allergies were always fucking up. I didn't even text him back; for what? To piss myself off some more. I already had class with Mrs. Ortiz's rude ass first thing in the morning. While I was pouting, he was texting me. The first text read: "Man chill out, you will see me today." [I ignored it] The following text said, "Ima come get you from school before 3rd period," and I was nervous.

All week, Vince hinted that he wanted my pussy. I wanted him too, but I had tried to have sex with my first love, 'Red', but he couldn't get it in. I tell you: I loved this boy since the 4th grade. I was willing to try because he was relocating over 1000 miles away. I didn't love Vince like I loved Red, and I didn't want a bad encounter, like with Red. A week before we fucked, I told Vince I was a virgin; Vince had fucked before, plenty of times. Scared, he told me, "I promise it's gonna feel good." I knew he was lying. But he said, "I wanna taste that pussy."

He asked me if I ever received head, or oral sex, before and I informed him that I had. He called me (surprised by my text, I guess) and said, "Now how the fuck is that possible?" I explained to him that the first time someone tasted me, I was well underage. Concerned, he asked had I ever been raped. Immediately, I shut down - I didn't feel comfortable anymore. 'Rape' is a trigger word for me. Escaping his question, I told him, "I will write a book about my life one day...just let me get some years on me, for closing chapters." He hung up on me and I could tell he was pissed off. I texted him and told him, "I was playing truth or dare with some of them project kids, and when I was 10-years-old, someone dared me to go in the closet with them when everyone went to sleep. I agreed and (while in the closet) the person asked if could they eat my coochie."

He told me I play too much and called me 'gay' of course, but that wasn't stopping shit. Everything we talked about ran through my head. I still wasn't ready, but I wanted to feel some type of pain. 'Nervous' should have been my middle name. He was outside waiting and I ran to the car. After I got in, I immediately started talking shit.

"Don't hurt me and if I say stop, stop!" I instructed. He laughed and told me to relax. He played my favorite 'Pretty Ricky' song and it made me want to take my panties off and put them in his mouth -except I didn't wear panties that day. We pulled up to his house and we went into his room; I started to undress, but he stared at me the whole time. Trying to make myself comfortable, I walked around to the left side of the bed, got under the covers and then I undressed – I just took off my pants. Shy and crazy, I left my sweater on and my jacket. He looked at me like: "bitch get naked" but he just said, "Earlissa, man take that shit off so we can make this happen." I replied, "Boy come on, before I change my mind."

'My, my, my' (*if you've ever been to church, then you've heard that lady in the back saying that, followed by the horn*) I'm glad his parents were at work because I screamed. He covered my mouth and said, "That's one way to get the neighbors knocking." Trying to relax, I spread my legs open and let him continue to finger me and I think to myself: if his fingers feel like this, what damage is his dick going to do?! He began laughing while going down to eat my pussy, and not knowing what he was laughing for, I closed my legs while his head was positioned between them, closing him up as well. He laughed even harder and by this time, I'm heated, so I'm screaming his middle name: 'Wayne,' and he says, "Stop playing let me suck that pussy." I released him (and my muscles), and laid back down.

He placed his hands under my ass, lifted me up and kissed my inner thighs. He then grabbed my knees as if he knew they would give out, and with his tongue, he started a tornado -slow licks and fast slurps. Putting his tongue deeper in my hole, I kicked the air until he stopped. I couldn't stop shaking. He asked me if I still wanted to fuck. I said, "Yes, let me feel you." He replied, "Shit, are you alright? Are you going to stop shaking?" I grabbed and pulled him closer, and then I grabbed his dick to put it inside.

I felt something piercing through me. I quickly pulled off that fucking jacket. I wasn't sure if I was up for the pain and I'm sure my facial expressions mirrored my nerves. He ensured me that I was super wet, and he just didn't want to hurt me. I said, "Get it over with." He shook his dick, then he slapped his dick on my pussy three times, and finally forced it in. I slapped him in his face because I was NOT expecting that much pain. He stroked slow and I couldn't do anything but lie there; I definitely felt him – he had a big dick. I was holding my stomach because the way he was fucking me, you could see him in my guts.

The more uncomfortable I was, the more he enjoyed it. He started fucking me extra hard and my shakes came back. I seriously had to hold my right leg down. He said, "Earlissa, I'm about to cum." I replied sharply, "Well cum on me not in me."

"I really don't want to get out of you," he explained. I wanted him to bust already. When he came, he made the ugliest face while shooting his sins all over my stomach. I touched it [the released sperm] because I never felt it before; it was warm and thick. He cleaned me up, and I put my clothes on ready for him to take me back to school. I was sitting on the edge of the bed and he comes up to me, picks me up and kisses me. I was pissed and ready to go. I had five different attitudes all because I wanted to be grown and fuck.

As we're in the car, I texted my best friend Todd and told him what happened. He [Vince] said, "Shit, you telling your friends I'm about to tell my niggas." Dialing his homeboy number, he says, "Yeah I'ma bout to tell them that you got that super soaker! You was so wet, I thought you peed on me." I started crying. I was embarrassed. He went on, "Shut yo' crybaby ass up, I didn't even call nobody." I don't even know why I was crying. I got back to the school, and my ride was already there. I didn't care about being seen; I was in so much pain that all I wanted to do was sleep.

I got home and fixed me and my siblings a snack and got in the bed. I tossed and turned all night. Around midnight, I noticed I was spotting. I tried to wake up my 'second parents', but they didn't come home that night. I texted Vince and he called when he was getting ready for school. He asked how I was doing and I couldn't even stand. I told him I wasn't really able to move and my parents hadn't come home. I stayed in the bed until noon and when my parents did arrive, my mother and I looked the same: like we just got fucked by a demon. My pops (Money) looked at me like he knew something but never said anything. My little brother Que said, "Dang sis, did you have sex last night?"

I ignored him and I began to text Vince. I was making plans to fuck again.

Sensational Surrender

I wasn't experimenting or anything, but I don't consider myself to be gay; because I don't eat pussy, but that's beside the point. She was a friend. How that changed, I don't know. We were joking around one night, and I knew she was bisexual - and whatever I chose to label myself. [A gay motherfucker knows a gay motherfucker.]

Finally, she got tired of the games and she said, "You need to stop playing and let me come pick you up and eat that pussy." I thought she was joking, but even if she was serious, I was ready; I had just showered and I was putting on bed clothes. I was so excited but nervous at the same time. That was not the first time I let a woman eat me out. I was 17 and she was 19 or 20. I didn't know if she wanted me to taste her back or finger her. I was clueless, but more than ready.

Me and Vince had ended it for good. Honestly, he's the one that told me she was gay. I was super horny; I had butterflies, but I got tired of waiting. I was like, "fuck it, she's not coming." I texted her and said, "Fuck it, I'm going to bed. You ain't coming, I'll hit you tomorrow." Immediately, she called me and she was like, "Shut the fuck up I'm on your street, but my blind ass can't find the house." I turned on the light and she pulled in.

I get into the car and it's completely silent. I was so nervous;my wetness could have been easily mistaken for urine. I sat there quietly. She started driving towards Lynwood and she drove down Parkdale to another street that lead to a little building. It was pitch black over there and all you could hear were dogs barking. That bitch was familiar with this spot, come to think about it. We parked and she said, "Get in the back." I climbed over the seat while she got out and got in. This bitch was super thick; she had little titties, flat stomach, big thighs and a big booty. That ho' [her ass] was stupid fat! I watched her get in; she was so sexy man - pretty as hell too. She got in the backseat, and I was leaned back like a nigga waiting on some head.

She rubbed my thighs, but stopped after 30 seconds. She made me feel ticklish. I pushed the negative thoughts far back in my brain: I know same-sex is a sin, but so is sex before marriage! I wanted her to explore my body, but she chose to fuck with my mind. She would touch me, then stop. I don't know if she was as nervous as I was, or trying to find my boundaries. Either way, I wasn't in the mood for her games. I smacked my lips and demanded to be taken home. She said, "Okay, lay back." I said, "Nah take me-," and that's all I got out because she dived in my pussy.

She was arched perfect. She wouldn't let me touch her; I wanted to smack her ass, suck her titties or something, but she held me down. That girl's whole mouth was on my pussy. She did some shit where she just used her lips; she glided her lips up and down. When she decided to use her tongue, she used her fingers as well. Tongue rolling slow, while her fingers were going slower. She sucked on my clit, started moaning and put her face deeper. She grabbed my thighs so I couldn't run; I tried to run. She pulled me in and sucked my pussy. I felt myself cumming and I thought I was possessed; I jumped up while still laying back and put my pussy in her throat, damn-near. She sucked my pussy so good that when she was done, I didn't move until she dropped me off. She bragged, and she earned that right. She became my lady after that.

Lil' Mexico (Jeffery)

Lil' Mexico (Jeffrey) set the bar high. We were too toxic though. Sex was great. In the midst of the lies, cheating, and fighting… sex was above all. At one point, [I believe] we loved sex with each other more than we loved each other. We went together in high school and never fucked so there was no waiting game really. I shot him a text: "Let me see your dick." This motherfucker really sent it! He joked that he hit it on the first night, which is half-ass true or all the way true depending on how you look at it; we had been talking for a while, but he was right, because after he sent the picture, I wanted to fuck him. I did fuck him.

Before we got to that point, we both talked our little shit, "I'ma do this'" "I know my shit good," etc., you know. I did/do it because I know what I got and what I'm capable of.

The first round, I did everything I said I was going to do. I think I said something like, "Yo dick ain't gonna be able to stand up in my pussy for long. On God stop playing with me." He knew he had to redeem himself because, no! – It wasn't bad at all, but I don't do quickies. He got up and he said,"let's go get in the bed." I got the best head ever that night – and many mornings and nights after. That nigga still top 5. But anyways, then this motherfucker flipped me over and started licking my ass. [Talk about singing love songs.]No, this wasn't the first time I've had my ass ate, but it was so much passion behind it, that I could have cried! And I mean he licked me real slow and it was soft, and he kissed my pussy. I said, "You put your tongue there stick a finger in," (talking about my ass). Then, he started spanking me. I started shaking as he's sitting there. He wrapped his arm around me, but under my stomach – while he has a finger in my ass and massaging my pussy with another, while sucking on my pussy. I guess we said, "Fuck them paper thin walls," because while I was cumming, I was screaming. Still ready for more (both of us),he said, "Now come ride this dick, bitch." I don't know why, but that shit turned me on even more! I jumped up on that fat dick and I slightly choked him (because 'bitch,' watch your mouth). That nigga had his grill in and he was just smiling. I'm looking down on him, fucking him while saying, "fuck me back" he was no little nigga. 'Big boy' was throwing dick – round 2! Somehow, we ended up cumming together and after that, we broke all the rules to the 'player handbook' (if there ever was one): I fell asleep in this man's bed, and he held me and let me rest. This was all on the first night! The rules were already broken,so why not continue to fuck em' up. We talked all day the next day.

That night, I decided I was going to cook him dinner. Sex from the night before had us on some new level shit! I went to his apartment. I knew role play was his shit, so why not make this shit happen already?! I arrived in a see-through tank top, some boy shorts that look like they were painted on and some thigh high black boots with a 5-inch heels. He slid the glass door open and said, "Oh, yeah?" That night, I was Sara; we both just laughed. He reached for the bag, but I yanked it and let him know in my George Lopez voice, "I got this!" As I'm walking to the kitchen, I got the feeling he was fucking me in his head. The stares he was giving melted me from behind. I sat the sack down and before I could grab anything out the sack, I felt his breath on my neck. It was warm, and I brushed up against him to let him know I knew he was there. He licked my ear then he grabbed my pussy and got on his knees, and started talking to my pussy. He said, "You're ready to be fucked, I smell you." He kissed my pussy through my panties. I'm not talking about a peck, I'm talking licking my pussy – deep-kissing my pussy. I was so wet, he started sucking my juices through my panties. I am not lying; I fucking lost it! I felt my knees giving out, so I moved to the counter for support. Not allowing me to catch my breath, he grabs my ass. I slowly started making my ass jump and he slapped my ass; I love that shit! He could tell by my reaction, and he slapped me even harder the next time.

"Smack it again!" I said, and he did and laughed, saying "Yo' ass freaky, stop playing! Do you want me to help you cook?" he asked. I started to let him, but I was there for sex and here we were falling in love. I was like, "No, give me a minute, and I'll be in there to suck yo' dick though." And he knew me, so he knew that was major because everybody don't get their dick sucked. I didn't even try to suck dick until I was 18 [so I'm really in this man kitchen cooking for him – on some king shit]. I asked him what he wanted before I got there, and he got just what he asked for. I'm rushing, but I'm not showing it. Finally, the food is on and I make him stand up. I don't suck dick on my knees, my knees are for praying only (he will tell you that)! I take his shorts off and before I pulled his dick out, I smelled the front of his boxers to make sure they didn't smell like piss. He laughed because he knew what I was doing. I caught him in the middle of his laughter (I was already slowly but quickly pulling his dick out) and I had my tongue out, so I let the tip of his dick touch it, then I grabbed his dick with my teeth and told him to come closer. I ran my hands up the side of his thighs before placing a grip on him. I slid my hand up his back and placed it in the middle of his back, because when I had him in the right position, I was going to eat that dick. I started sucking his dick. He let his head fall back. He's enjoying it, and so am I. I expressed my feelings for the dick through moans and I told him to talk to me (I still had his dick in my mouth). He backed up and looked at me, so I pushed him down on the couch and gave that nigga 'cookie monster' kisses to the dick. 'Nummmmnummmnmm,' followed by sounds that

sounded like, 'ssssslllllllluuuuuuuuuppppppp'
'pppppppppppppooooooopppp' – I was face deep in his
lap; eating dick and jacking him off when my jaws got tired.
He laid me down and he was rough, but gentle. He knew to
lean on me, to apply more pressure. I don't care, I don't
care; we made love that night, we had sex... we also
fucked – all over the floors.

Up against the walls, he slowly kissed me, and I don't
do kisses like that. That night, anything was okay – straight
'go mode.' I licked his lips then he said, "Give me your
tongue." Not giving a fuck about everything we just done, I
stuck my tongue out and he licked the top and bottom of
my tongue; I caught his tongue and slowly sucked it. I've
never been turned on like this. He felt my body jumping,
and he began to play in my pussy – I became silly putty.
He stuck his fingers in, and started to go in-and-out real
fast. He stuck his fingers in about 20 times and on the 21st
insertion, he hooked his fingers inside of me and pushed
on the gate that was holding the flood. He watched me
squirm, scream, cream and pour out like a firefighter hose.
Embarrassed as fuck, I put my face in a pillow. He got up
and he cleaned us both up. He kissed my forehead, and
then my pussy. We set up and we talked for hours. I slept
in his arms like we owed it to each other.

A few days later, he picked me up for our first date. We spent the day in Lawton. We became closer and closer no longer caring who we once belonged to. He had a girlfriend (she didn't stay here) and I was single, but hurting from a past relationship. Over the next 4 and a half years, we had tried a little bit of everything. From me jacking him off with my feet, to letting each other cum on one another to upside-down '69'. My foot got caught in the ceiling fan that night. After a while, sex was our drug of choice. We could tear the whole house up fighting, but you 'best believe' we were fucking, once all that shit got picked up. There wasn't and isn't a cure for sex to me. The more I have sex, the more I crave it. I knew I was addicted when I cried for my fix, and I just got a dose. Sex is a hell of a drug; sex, love and pain have always been the strongest drugs I've consumed.

Masturbation Part 1

With all the years I've dealt with my sex addiction, I never masturbated until I was 27. (Crazy... I know) I have my reasons for not masturbating. First, for me, it's a sin (in the 'freaks' only bible, as well). I'm so freaky, I just think, "that's why God made sex partners and/or a mate." Second, I love my wetness, but I don't like it on me. After my 5 year relationship ended, I had no choice but to at least give it a try.

If I go without sex, my pussy throbs and then it gets fatter. I even start shaking and immediately I tighten my muscles. One time it got so bad, I slept with an ice pack between my legs. The old me would have texted an old hoe from my past, but the new me has self control and ahold of my addiction; to the point where although I crave, it I don't have to go get it.

A shared video of me dancing in some stripper shoes popped up on my Facebook memories, and a girl named Nicole hit me up. She asked basic questions [You know: age, occupation, attachments, etc] and we exchanged numbers. So as she got my number, she texted me and questioned whether I was lesbian or bisexual. I started to not text back, but I texted her

back and explained to her that I was bisexual, I suppose – she
asked me what did I mean by that. What I meant was: I've had
three girlfriends in my life and over 5 women have tasted me
but I don't return the favors.

I explained to her my reasons and for a minute, it just got
quiet. When she finally decided to talk again, she asked me if I
pleasured myself. Yes, I knew she was a lesbian, but got damn
this wasn't 21 questions – and hell no I didn't touch myself! I
said, "Hell no, I ain't never been that lonely." My answer
pissed her off. "I play with my pussy four times a day
sometimes, and ain't shit wrong with it, "she said. I laughed
because she raised her voice like she knew me about fingers in
a pussy.

She said, "Don't laugh at me, I want to ask you something."
Still laughing, I said, "What's up lady?" Nicole asked me if I
would pleasure myself for her. I said, "Bitch, I'm about to
hang up! I've never had phone sex either....I'm a real freak."

"If you are a real freak, you'll fuck me over the phone," Nicole
said. She was really getting on my nerves so I said, "If you can
turn me on, I'll make you bust." This girl said, "No I can't, I'm
at work." So I told her, "Right now, tell me you want to eat my
pussy." She laughed and replied, "I really do wanna do that."
"Do what?" I asked. "You gotta say it, or I'm not gone lay the
phone by my pussy so you can get that surround sound", I told

her. She put on her sexy voice and said, "I want you to meet me in my king size bed and just lay there, and let me suck on you until you are ready to cum. Then when you get ready to cum, ride my face -so all your juices go to the back of my throat." My pussy heard every word!

I was already soaked and creaming from all the teasing. Closing my legs, trying not to give in, I accidentally let out the moan I was holding in. She said, "Keep going, I can't hear you. I'm about to put in my headphones and you can get as loud as you want." This would be my first time, so hell – I didn't even know how loud I would be.

I was so horny, so I started with one finger. I took my index finger and slowly rubbed my drizzling clit, then sucked the juices off. Turned on by my taste, my pussy started throbbing; I started breathing hard. I'm not use to being this horny - and not fucking afterwards. I placed the phone down and got two fingers. I jammed both fingers in, and went in-and-out of my pussy really hard. Nicole is texting me, coaching me on what to do next. I start rubbing the hood of my pussy in circular motion.

I didn't want to enjoy it as much as I did. She could hear it in the way I started to pant, that I was about to cum. I was so ready. I was turned on by my wetness, the sound (the music, rather) and my moans – it just all ran together; one of the sweetest love songs one can make by themselves. She said, "Don't cum yet." Squirming, trying to find words to say, I told her I needed to while she was texting the way she wanted me on her face. She was also making the sounds through the phone and talking real nasty, but I was fucking myself, listening and reminiscing about the night that one chick sucked my pussy so good, I had to make sure I had my ass attached to me.

She said, "Ask me, can you cum." I heard her lock her office door. Ready to get her started, I told her, "No, but send me a picture of that pussy, I know you wet." She replied "I'm already three steps ahead of you baby!" I checked my phone. I was shocked to see Bella had texted me. I opened that first and, going back into the conversation with Nicole, I asked, "Can I cum now?" Before she could answer, I came everywhere. No longer interested in what Nicole was saying, I just hung up the phone.

Bella was super sexy and freaky – I never touched this woman. The nude she sent was amazing! 'Omg' she had a bob haircut with blue tips, beautiful brown eyes, clear lip gloss, lashes on, white toes and a tattoo on her stomach. She wanted to video chat so I told her to give me a minute. She said, "I already know you ain't got no clothes on, so I'm about to call you." She called and when I answered the video chat, I had my camera on my pussy; she loved to see my insides – no lie, I got a pretty pussy.

She talked to my pussy until she could see it jumping, and the cream started playing peek-a-boo. I begged her to stop before I squirted on my phone. She said, "Lissa, I know you don't want a relationship, but I just want to be able to please you when I want – I want a pussy like yours in my life. Let me come see you and bring you flowers." I wanted her, but I couldn't please her the way I knew she would please me....

Marqus

"Come to room 215," I texted Marqus. This motherfucker shouts: "Is this you with this butt pad and unnecessary weave?" I shouted back, "Fuck you boy!" I kept it short because Erin and Madison were standing right there. The girls walked in and I stayed behind and whispered, "I'ma make you eat it just because you said that." He laughed as we walked in and said, "I'm going to eat off yo' back side because I want to." We chilled with the girls before he had to go. He had a bachelor party he was hosting, but he was coming back to spend the night. I knew it would be late so I gave him a room key. I wasn't waiting up for no dick, I had 'family day' planned for my kids,plus my parents' room were two doors down.

My kids went to work-out with my mom. After I smoked and showered, I was in the bed and it was only 8 o'clock. He called me and told me he was going to stop by to drop off his stuff. I fell asleep, but I heard the door open. I looked at the clock and it was only 10:33PM. Knowing who it was, I didn't even rollover. I heard him sit his bag down, but I didn't hear him come to the bed. He pulls me from under the cover, and lifts up my bed shirt and starts eating my pussy. Giving me sloppy head but neatly performed. He had me scratching the bed or running - whatever you want to call it. He started sucking the inside of my pussy as if his lips were the straw, and my nectar was store brought in a can. To top it off, he spread my flower and gave me 1000 kisses.

It had gotten really good to him; he got down on his knees. He hadn't made it to the club yet, and most of the time, he dressed like a businessman. I told him to get up (I didn't want him on his knees, yet. Plus, I didn't want to mess up his clothes). He said, "After all these years, you've still got it!" I looked at him and told him to 'get out' because that was just stupid. Around three o'clock, I heard him getting out the shower. He peeked to see if I had woken up since he been there, and of course, my childish ass was playing sleep with my eyes low, wondering if he was going to come out the bathroom naked. He got in the bed shivering, trying to get under me. He was dry, but his body was still cold. He said, "I know what will warm me up!"

Before I could ask him what he meant, he was jumping out the bed walking to the foot of the bed. Crawling under the covers, he spread my legs and now he could get messy, I spread my legs even wider – both of my feet on a different edge of the bed. He sucked on my pussy really quick and backed off. He waited a minute, then he licked on me real slow while rubbing my thighs before placing his hands under me. I said, "Now eat that pussy!" I began to tell him how nasty he was, and he flicked his tongue real fast on my clit. I was so turned on, I went under the cover with him.

I couldn't take any more tongue, so I grabbed his dick and told him that I needed to feel him.

I love when Marqus fucks me missionary first. It's like a warm up to our sex sessions [and positions]. He placed his hands in the bed as if he was punching the bed and started doing push-ups while he was slapping dick inside of me. He's a talker. There's nothing wrong with that, but here we are fucking eight years later – don't ask me if you're 'still the best I ever had.' Hating to be ignored, he thrusted harder in me and instructed: "Talk to me." He was drunk and getting on my nerves. I said, "Could you shut the fuck up and suck my pussy!?" He said, "All you gotta do is ask, you know I got you! He stuck his arms under my thigh and brought my pussy to his face he said, "Now serve me so I can shut up."

I asked him for permission to cum on his face. He moaned and opened his mouth wider before answering me. He answered, "Girl, I've been letting you cum in my mouth since the first time...why wouldn't you be able to cum on my face? Stop playing and squirt on me!" I love when he talks to me like that. Normally, I am afraid to gush or squirt because 'me being me,' if I were a nigga and a woman did that to me, I would be upset, and one of us would have to go. He claimed, "I like when you wet me up." I'm looking at him while he's saying this in between him eating my pussy – he looked so innocent eating my pussy. His soul was crying. "Somebody ain't been feeding my baby right," I thought. I grabbed his head and brought him in closer and told him to open his mouth wide and I came in his mouth (just a little, for him to taste) and told him to, "...Get up and fuck me from behind."

He laid there for a few seconds like he didn't want to, so I slipped from under him and when I got up, his head was still in my pussy area. I climbed up his face – I didn't want to ride his face, I just wanted to leave a trail of me on his face. Dragging me back down, I left a trail from his forehead to his stomach. Kissing him from his forehead to his stomach, then licking him from his forehead to his stomach… and I sat on his dick. He fucked me from the bottom to the point where I had to just lay there and take his dick (I just needed a minute to gather myself). I let him take control just because I'm a 'pain-freak.' *The more pain, the better...* I will always say that.

He said, "Oh, before I forget, I owe you something," I already knew what he was talking about, but I acted as if I didn't know. I replied, "What daddy!?" He advised: "Get up and put that ass in my face!" I pushed him to his knees right off the bed – he was drunk as fuck, he didn't mind. I told him to remain still and I got on the bed and got on all fours. He locked his arms in between my legs, pretzel-shaped, and I moved to the edge of the bed and kept my ass up. I put my face in the pillow, grabbed my ass and opened it for him, and he kissed me from my ass to my pussy. Then he licked my pussy from the back before he stuck his tongue deep in my ass. Screaming in the pillow crying to the sex gods, he kept going and he said, "Shake that ass all on me!" Honestly, I didn't know how he was even still breathing.

We cut up for no reason, I needed some more dick though. I said, "Fuck me real hard, I need to feel you." He wiped his face, rubbed his dick and put his dick in me. I was throwing it back so hard, he lost his balance, but his dick never came out; he fucked me harder and harder. He said, "Tell me you love me, girl." I replied, "I love this dick, keep fucking me!" He smacked his lips and called me by my first name (of course I didn't answer him). After a minute, he said [while bursting], "You know I love you girl and I'm in love with this pussy." I would say [bursting], 'in me,' but it was a condom he had burst in (not taking away from the feeling).

Hearing him moan the way he did, made me cum in the middle of his cummings. He took the condom off and stripped the first layer of sheets, telling me how he forgot how messy I can get. After he fixed the bed, he told me he was going to sleep. I'm not going to bed wet and sticky like that; I went to run my shower. I came out to grab my towel and he was snoring; I was only in there long enough to make sure the shower was clean and that my water was hot and he was knocked out! He felt me sit on the bed and he had the nerve to ask me did *he go to sleep*. Shortly after, he went right back to sleep – dick on hard.

I turned on the TV because I couldn't go back to sleep – I had already slept over five hours. He woke up at 6:45AM, grabbed a condom from under his pillow and said, "I had a dream that I was fucking you. Making love while the sun was waking up the earth." I don't remember the time I passed out, but I was getting a room call at 10:00AM from my mom, asking why Marqus took the girls for breakfast and why I was still in bed. I checked my phone and Marqus texted me when the girls came and knocked on the door. He was already up, dressed and cleaning up. I got my 'sexed-out' ass up out the bed, rolled up, showered and got ready for the day. It was another day filled with endless events for the family and when the night came, we sexed it away before I had to head back to Wichita Falls the next morning.

What Goes Around

"You look like you got some good pussy…" I'm sitting next to this dude I met two days ago, and he already talking out his neck. I'm sure my black ass turned bright red. Anybody that knows me knows I'm rude, yet very shy at times and I'm always nervous. I'm trying not to laugh or entertain him, but he said, "I want you to get my chin wet."

I said, "Oh my God please stop." I'm looking around the room, making sure I'm the only one that could hear him; he was not whispering. Here we are sitting in the training room. There are five people present including the trainer. It was so quiet, you could hear a roach snatching crumbs.

He said, "Come sit on my lap." I ignored him and he asked, "Who you at work looking good for?" I asked him to 'please stop,' while laughing. We go outside for a break and I take off my hoodie and he's walking behind me and exclaims, "Damn girl you got a lil' drop back there." I told him to shut up. I told him to stop saying all that shit in the [training] class, because the whole call center looked at us like we've been fucking. He said, "Fuck them! They just want to fuck me, but I always be around you… so that must mean I'm trying to be the one to fuck you."

Speechless, I just started walking back towards the building. He watched me walk away because he told me when we got back to class that I was 'bowlegged' (which I thought I'd grew out of). Out of nowhere, he insisted, "Try me one time. You're going to love my dick. I don't like to do a lot of talking, I'd rather show you. "I said, "Be quiet, I'm really trying to learn." He's next to me now, and he advised me to look down. I don't know why, but I looked down at his private area. Obviously, that's what he wanted me to do. He pulled the right side of his shorts up to where it tightened around his thigh, and this man's dick was so thick and long. I stared at it – I really stared at it. I started having visions of fucking him on the table. I told him to stay away from me because he would be trouble for real. He laughed and told me I was scary. I wasn't scared, I just didn't want another person knowing me deep like that at the moment.

Over the next few weeks, we became closer. At this point, everybody thought we were fucking. If they were looking for him at work, they would ask me – I didn't even have his number. We were work best-friends. I'm lying around the house writing and I got a text around 4am saying: "I know you're up, do you wanna match?" I don't smoke everybody weed. I texted him back and told him that I had some gas to put in a backwood; "…just come over and we can smoke in my car," I insisted. He pulled up 30 minutes later, and as I'm rolling, up he says, "I think you're scared of me." I laughed and looked at him like: 'bitch please!' I told him, "I'm not them other bitches you've fucked… I know what I got so let's not go there." He went on, "I'm just saying, I bet you won't climb on this motherfucker (talking about his dick)." I told him, "I would, but we shouldn't cross those lines… because the energy we send off together would be poison, and I don't want to ruin a good friendship."

I fired up the blunt, trying to deaden the conversation. I passed him the blunt and this nigga has got his dick out, stroking it (before now, I only had seen his dick through his shorts). I reached over and grabbed his dick. When I touched his dick, it was Deja-vu.

Not sure of the lifetime, but I *knew* this dick too well. He handed off the blunt with his right hand and with his left hand, he tapped on my thigh and my legs parted like the Red Sea. He looked me in my eyes and asked me if he could touch me. My body begged for him – with his mind, he had already fucked me. Reading my thoughts and answers, he slid his finger down my clit.

He said, "…and you weren't going to let me get none of this!? You're selfish." "I don't think we're ready for each other," I replied. He stuck his finger in me and pulled it out, and stuck it in his mouth. His eyes still locked with mines he said, "Yeah I'ma need this pussy…" I put the blunt out. I climbed over and sat on his dick. He said, "Oh yeah, you're a freak… I can tell by the way you climbed on that thang!" I sat there for a minute because it hurt, and I jumped on it like it didn't. I had one foot on the cup holder and the other on the door and I started jumping up and down on his dick. The harder our bodies smashed together, the harder his dick got and my juices flowed. I put my feet down, I needed to feel the pain you receive when the dick is standing up inside you.

He started to grind his hips and I leaned up a little. I needed him to fuck me – fuck that slow shit. We were in-sync already; as soon as I leaned up, he followed up by grabbing my waist and yanking my head back. He stopped, so I started throwing it back, fucking him. He said, "Stop girl, I don't wanna cum." I jumped off his dick, leaving us both wanting more! We finished smoking, and we talked a little more before we parted ways. The next morning, he texted me and was like: "Man I've been thinking about that pussy all night!" I texted him back and told him that was just a sample. He asked me when would we fuck again. I told him that was it, I didn't want to make it a habit. He called me later that night to see if I was up. I was, but we've already crossed the lines that we shouldn't. He texted me every other day just to check on me.

After two weeks, I reached out to him and we met up for lunch. As the wait staff is seating us, this fool says, "She tryna keep that good pussy from me." I told him we'd fuck soon. Hell, I worked three jobs and I didn't have time for dick like that. I don't fuck if I'm not in a relationship, because the dick isn't always guaranteed and I come from having sex every day: morning head, lunch sex, nightly fuck sessions and feeding my nigga ass cakes for a midnight snack. I informed him that I was just holding out because I knew me, and there was no need to wake a demon I could barely control. He laughed and said that I think too much and I need to just live! After lunch, I went back to work and I decided the next time we fucked, I was going to fuck his head up.

A week later, he sent me a video of him lying in bed and his big dick was just dangling everywhere. He was laying there with his blue sheets, skinny, naked body and dick. I watched the videos about three times. I liked the way his sins shot out then ran down his dick like a volcano. He said, "Come get yo' dick!" I went to his apartment and I rolled up, listening to him call me a 'stranger.' Shit, I wasn't trying to be a stranger, but I was already balancing a household with two kids, three jobs and writing a book. I told him I didn't come over his place to hear that shit. I came to fuck and chill. He laid on the couch and told me to come lay with him. I got under the cover and laid under him… immediately, his dick got hard.

"See what you do to me girl?" He began to put his dick between my ass cheeks. "I'm about to get naked – fuck this, I wanna feel your warm skin," he said, while yanking at his drawstring on his sweatpants. He got up off the couch to take his clothes all the way off. I stretched out so the only place to lay was on me. Standing on the side of the couch in front of me, he grabbed my legs and put them over the edge of the couch, causing me to fold. He was turned on even more for the simple fact he knew I was flexible. He came and got between my legs after pulling them straight in the air. It's been two months since we fucked and he wanted me to feel it. He was not gentle at all. He was fucking me saying, "Don't keep this pussy from me. Anytime I want this pussy, you're supposed to let me satisfy you."

I was silent because this man was in my guts and wouldn't let up. But I don't tap out ever. He said, "I like how your pussy so tight right now!" He just jumped up and pulled out. I looked up to see what the issue was and he said, "You know your pussy good man!" (He was nutting on the floor) I said, "I know you not finished, because that will piss me the fuck off… you didn't even say you were about to cum." He replied, "You was right, your pussy is not like what I'm used to. But, I'm good… come sit on this dick." Even harder, his dick was right back in my pussy. I was trying to position myself on his dick and he started fucking me. I fucked him back, but told him to 'stop' cause I wanted to fuck him. Both facing forward, I reached back and put my hands behind his head and slowly grinded on him. In return, he reached around me and grabbed my titties, and ran his hand down my stomach to my pussy. I lifted up on my tip toes and placed my hands on his thighs so I wouldn't lose my balance. I wanted him to ram his dick inside of me. I spread my ass cheeks and slammed myself to him and locked like dogs.

I don't know what I was thinking, but out of nowhere, I stopped fucking him and made my ass clap on his dick before I jumped down on it. Coming up off the dick, I made my ass shake in small circles, then I would jump back down on it. He said, "Hell nah, man. You're not just gone do my shit like that. Let's go to the bed." I lead the way to his bed, I still had my hair wrap and shirt on – he followed behind ass naked. I made him lay down – I wasn't finished, but soon as I got on top, he rolled me on my back and he still had his left arm under my back and stroked me back-to-back. There really wasn't a speed to it, though. It slowed my heart rate and we started to have sex, instead of fuck. My body... it was sensitive to a[ny] touch, a sweet nothing, oxygen, thoughts, etc. Everything at the moment turned my body on! It was like the more we fucked on each other in that bed, the hornier I became. Crazy shit, he felt it, too, and he was ready to bust. He didn't want to get too attached he wanted to leave me wanting more.

I'm not complaining, but I wasn't finished. I came four times but there were no orgasm(s). My body isn't satisfied without an 'O'. He said, "I want to fuck you some more, but I'm about to bust." He jumped up and came in his hand. He cleaned me up and I put my pants on and left. "You gonna come over here, and mess up my sheets and leave," he said as I was walking out. I texted him and told him he was being stingy with his dick and we weren't fucking any more. He texted me back: "…you said that last time."

"I promise you'll hit me up before I text you," I shot back. He replied, "You try to run shit too much and I'm a man… blah

blah blah…." He tried to be stingy with his dick. I'm not submissive to a motherfucker that I'm just fucking. I understand a man wanting to be dominant, but you will always play by my rules. For weeks on end, he texted things like: "you must be back with yo' nigga," "…are you for real," "…I didn't even get to put my mouth on you," "…why you acting like that?" "Come get this dick," "Just come smoke with me, I'll behave." I didn't wanna hear none of that shit; I didn't like how the last session ended. I finally texted him: "send me a picture of that big dick." He texted back and asked why I didn't already have one, but I didn't reply… so he just sent the picture. I went back to not talking to him. I got a friend request from him on FaceBook and I accepted it. He messaged me: "You up on FaceBook? Come over for a little, I got my son, and I think he's around your kids, age. He needs kids to play with while he's here, and I need a playdate with you."

I messaged him back and told him that he didn't want a playdate with me, because I was only willing to fuck him one last time. I told him, "I know I said that shit last time, but my mind is really made up." He replied, "Come over tonight and I'll make it right." The day I left, I knew we only had one last session left in us, and I was running the show. I decided to make him wait. He started back with the messaging: "Good morning beautiful," (he only did that one other time)… "You've been a real friend to me and looked out for me, the least I can do is smoke with you, " I aint fucking nobody… I've been waiting on you," "You said I was stingy, and now I'm trying to give you some dick – you ignore me, but you give yo' time to other niggas." That text pissed me off because 'hold the fuck on!'

"Who said I had to chill with you and I'm single, but that gave you no right to try to charge me up. Please don't text me back, because you really gave me a headache," I texted him. He texted back and was like, "I didn't mean to offend you, I'm just saying you spend your time with the wrong nigga… being stressed out. I'm saying we can help each other; it's not all sex, we can be business partners." I didn't text back. He texted again and said, "So now you sleep!?" He started to get annoying and I told him I had a man so he should stop double-texting me. I really didn't [have a man] but he was bugging and as crazy as it sounds, it made his dick value go down for me. I honestly got mad because: 'don't hit my line like I got to answer you.'

I woke up the next morning still pissed, wanting to change my number. I hit him up and told him after he put his prince to sleep, to fuck with me. He replied, "Damn, you talking to me like you the nigga." I didn't reply. He hit me at 8:55AM. (Well nah, you not going to rush me) I texted him back around 10:30AM and asked him what he was doing. He was watching a movie and waiting on me so he could roll up. I pulled up at 11:20AM and the door was already unlocked, so I walked in, and he just looked at me. I came over in an olive green dress that stopped mid-thigh and some black Chuck Taylors. Simple, but enough to turn any person on. He asked me why did I come over like that and I explained: "easy access," right? He started pulling on his dick. I just got the vibe that his performance was going to be top notch, he was just too ready. Not that too ready soon as I feel you I'ma bust… but, that 'bitch I'ma make you take this dick for hiding and keep this good pussy away' ready.

I told him I didn't wanna smoke until after the first round; I love a motherfucker that can perform sober. When I say that, I mean no liquor, weed, pills or porn to help you bust that first one to last longer… just your body and an open mind. He goes down, attempting to devour my pussy (he had that devil look in his eyes as he opened my legs and saw my *labia minora* glazed). I stopped him because he didn't deserve to drink my alkaline water. Plus, this was the last time we would fuck, no need in doing something we haven't been doing if this is it. As I pulled him up, he kissed my thighs and laid me down. Thank God there was already a sheet laying down; I felt myself dripping and I grabbed the towel off the edge of the couch and started to wipe myself off – I was super wet and we hadn't fucked yet.

He raised his voice and asked me why did I do that [use that towel], when his mouth could have cleaned my wet spot. I wanted to shove his head in my pussy. I'm lying there ready to feel his pain. He yanked me up and said, "Fuck that, stand up. I ain't seen yo' ass in… I don't know how long, bend over!". I laughed while getting up so he pushed me over and slapped my ass. Anybody that knows me, knows that I love that shit! But we couldn't be too loud because his son was in the other room asleep. I told him to spank me and that I would be quiet. Feeling that *pleasurable-pain,* and having to remain silent had me creaming. I took his dick and rubbed it around the inside of me, just for a second – I just wanted him to see the mess we were creating. I then stuck my finger in my pussy so he could taste my cream pie. I sat down on the couch, opened my legs, showed him the cream close up and told him to fuck me already. He took his clothes off and got on top of me.

I grabbed him by his waist to feel him closer. He started fucking me and he said, "Girl, open up them legs." It took me a minute because he got the type of dick that, if you don't fuck it often, it rips you when you finally do… if you're not careful. He said, "I know it hurt, but you chose to keep yourself away from me. You know you're always welcome to this dick." The words worked like a spell, because my legs were open and he was stroking so deep, it was like he was hitting my tailbone. I started digging into his back and he started fucking me like he was cumming already, but the jerking actually made his dick hit the top and bottom walls of my pussy. I could still feel him in the middle, if that makes any sense. He stopped and looked at me. I knew he stopped because he didn't want to cum yet, but I started fucking him from under. I heard him say, "Stop, I don't wanna cum," but I kept fucking him anyways.

He gave short strokes, while trying to get to the long strokes without ending the round too soon. He jumped up and said, "Fuck this, I need to smoke. I'm trying to fuck you all night!" I exclaimed, "Noooo, I just want to fuck you twice and go home." "You said I was being stingy, well now I'm trying to give you all this dick," he said with a little attitude. I picked the blunt up and lit it and he played in my pussy, being childish by mocking the noise my pussy made. Embarrassed, I closed my legs and pushed him away. He said, "How you so freaky, but get shy and nervous like that around the person you're fucking?" I kissed him on his neck and sat in his lap. He's watching TV and I'm looking at the wall. He smelled my hair and I felt his dick thump against my ass.

I was sitting on his lap but I was up far enough to wet up his stomach. I start to get up, but you could see my wetness streaming off of me, sticking to him. He gave me that look and I sat down - reverse cowgirl style. With his dick in me, I bent over so he could see my pussy from the back on his dick. I grabbed his ankles, then I decided to just place my hands on the floor and I started at the bottom of his dick. No inch, centimeter or snap of dick left behind. I grinded on it slow to get the full effect of his manhood and it reminded me of the way a cowbell rolls around hitting everything on its insides. Then to feel maximum pain, I rode my way to the top. I was going to slide down his dick full speed, all-force, but he placed both hands on my titties and slammed me down himself — we both screamed. Bending back over, I arched my back low enough for him to have full control and to slowly turn this position into doggy style. He chokes me from behind and brings me up to his level fucking me harder and harder each time I throw it back.

I got so into it — my throwing it back turned into him just holding me and me fucking him (while still in our animal form). I told him to get up, I wanted to ride his dick, but he didn't sit down so I put one foot on the couch and climbed on his dick while he was still standing and he smiled. He grabbed my right leg and started fucking me back. That shit was driving me wild! He walked me to the wall and I bent back enough to balance us both on the wall so he could fuck me deeper. He whispered that he loved my pussy and I told him that I knew he did, but the way he said it caused my juices to run to the floor. He said, "Got damn, Lissa, you won't wet up my chin… but you're willing to wet up my feet." Laughing like always, I told him to shut up and fuck me.

Still holding me, he walks me over to the couch and he kissed me. Before placing me down he says, "I just want to make sure you leave her tonight satisfied, I don't want you to feel like you ain't doing enough because you are and I wasn't trying to be stingy with my dick… it just seemed like that's all you wanted from me and I'm more than just sex." I replied, "I understand that. Just because I ask you for sex doesn't mean that's all I want from you… but it's all I need from you."

His words (which pissed me off) didn't change that fact that this was the last time. He sat me down and told me to turn on my side; he got behind me and beat my pussy up from another angle. He fucked me faster for all the 'no's' I gave him, and he fucked me rougher for all the attitude I'd given. Choking me and placing his finger in my mouth, he kissed the back of my next and he whispered: "This really doesn't have to be the last time." I threw it back and smiled, remaining silent. He said, "Man, you like that shit... you know you've got some good pussy and you're gonna keep it away from me again." He rubbed my legs lifting them up one-by-one, kissing on them when he had the chance. He turned my neck around and kissed my lips again – this time, trying to add tongue. I let him kiss me again, but he was not about to stick his tongue in my mouth. I was thinking: "what's up with this kissing shit." It was throwing my whole mood.

I told him to pick another position and he said, "Come ride this dick before you try to burn off." I rode his dick with one leg on the back of the couch and the other on the floor he started to moan louder and shake, so I slowed down for him.

He asked me why do I be fucking him like that, if I'm not gone fuck him often. "YOU TRIED TO BE STINGY WITH THAT BIG DICK AND I TOLD YOU, YOU CAN'T FUCK WITH ME," I explained confidently. I jumped off his dick like he jumps out of my pussy and I laughed while he sat there with his dick in his hands. He said, "What the fuck, man!" I said, "I'm about to go home, I'm tired." "Just like that?" he asked. Not caring about him being upset I said, "Hell yeah! I just needed one more session with you and now we can be friends." I got up and kissed him on the forehead and told him to 'take care.' I locked the door and walked to [maybe] the third step, and he came out and told me to text him when I made it home – I kept walking like I didn't hear him. I got home 10 minutes later. I sat there for a minute thinking I was wrong, but he texted me in between my thoughts and said he would get used to not hearing from me again.

Bed, Frame, & Beyond

The bed came off the rails and landed completely on the floor tonight–but before we got to that point, I knew we were going to fuck some shit up [but not like that]. I wanted him all day,but there were a whole bunch of people around, plus the kids, so I stayed off to myself. I even left to go have a drink to ease my sexual desires. He was barbequing and I didn't want to just be under him as horny as I was. I went in the house to roll a blunt and he followed behind me asking me do I "...want some sausage?" He had just took the meat off the grill, but I didn't want that type of sausage:hot link,weenie, weiner, none of that – I wanted that dick.

Knowing we on the same level, I say, "Yeah I do, so stop playing." He sat the tray of food down and said, "Baby you're a freak! Stop playing before I bend yo' ass over in this kitchen and bust yo' ass down." I started laughing because I knew he was serious and (even with a yard full of people)I wouldn't have stopped him. As I'm leaning over the island in the kitchen he comes behind me and asked me what I wanted to do tonight. I turned around and kissed his lips, sucking on the bottom lip as I pulled away. He said, "So that's what you wanna do!?" I just looked at him because he knew I wanted some dick. He said, "Baby don't look like that (lost)." couldn't help it, I counted the days with him – our sex was so good.

He finally said the words I wanted to hear: "Baby I will give you some dick tonight!" Music to my soul! The way my body shifted positions without force,I could have came right then without being touched. We made plans to go drink later at the bar… nothing fancy. However, when I get horny and can't fuck right then, I tend to fall asleep. I don't know if it's because I refuse to pleasure myself, or if I'm just used to fucking when I want – as many times as I want; I was spoiled either way.

I keep my phone on silent because it is always going off [one call or text after another]. I got up at 10:36PM; my phone was ringing and it was my dude bitching. Yes, I told him I was coming to get my plates when he called at 8:15PM, but again, I went to sleep – shit I couldn't get no dick and [hell] that made me restless. I pulled up at midnight and he was pissed but, I honestly didn't care. I listened to him bitch and say how he wanted to "...go out and socialize" and shit. I noticed his dick getting hard through his shorts, growing – sitting up on his thigh like a king itself.

I'm nasty and I don't care. I reached under his shorts and grabbed it. That bitch so thick, I'd grab it in church. (I'm just being 100% Lissa right now, God already be watching so do not judge me!) I just started sucking it. I don't like spit anywhere – that's the biggest turn off during sex to me. So, I got some spit and just held it in the back of my throat so when I deep-throated him, it wouldn't hurt (although I don't mind a little pain), and as I'm going deep and deep-throating, swallowing him whole, he's fucking my mouth – and I let him. He draws back because at the same tempo, he would cum.

He said, "You gotta stop doing that shit [sucking his dick like that] because you don't be wanting to be this freaky every night." "Damn, I don't deserve a night off?" I asked him laughing like I do. He said, "You know you enjoy that shit." I do as well, but sometimes he be on punishment and don't acknowledge that shit at all. He asked, "Can I eat your pussy tonight?" I replied, "You can taste me." He always just dives in (he doesn't get to taste me too often) and 20 seconds in, I pulled him up. Not because I wasn't enjoying it, but I just wanted some dick.

He already knew to throw that dick in me with extra pain. I like to hear my pussy gushing when he pulls it after he sticks it in.

The first stroke induced pain, the second stroke brought relief and the strokes to follow… pure pleasure! Three different feelings at various speeds. We're fucking and he pulls out and puts his dick back in his shorts. [Pissed me the fuck off!] So, I sat up and looked him in his eyes and I sucked my finger and rubbed my clit. I opened up for him and he never looked back up, so I closed my legs. We both can play games.

      Remaining naked, I laid slanted on the right side of the couch ass poking out. Even though I never took my eyes off the TV, I seen him looking at me and stroking his dick. He pulled me but I pulled back because, "naaaaawwwwww nigga…." He said, "Why the fuck you wanna play and my dick hard." "Bitch your dick was hard when you was fucking me-" I sharply replied before he cut me off. "I was just teasing, but you're in here playing man...what the fuck, man!?" laughed because I'm not the one that started this whole show. I didn't see him walk up on me, but I suddenly felt a breeze and I looked up. When we made eye contact, he grabbed me by the throat and walked me to him. Caught off guard, I go with what he's doing. He sits down with his hand still gripped around my neck and he with his right arm he lifted my leg up and started sucking my pussy. That pain mixed with pleasure by mouth turned on a different freak in me. I felt myself about to splash, slowly climbing off his mouth and up his face. I kissed the top of his head before I slid down his face, neck, chest, and stomach. Taking his hand off my throat he said, "Grab the back of the couch." While I'm holding onto the couch, he lifts up both thighs and he holds me in the air and I know then, at any second, he's going to drop me. Talking his shit, he said, "Prepare yourself." This time I didn't laugh. We have no safe words so I undo my pony-tail and ran my left hand through my hair (14,16,18 deep wave). I slightly leaned forward and put my left hand behind his neck, right hand still holding the couch. I licked my lips and I said, "Go!" We touched so fast and so hard,I squirted on his dick. The pain... seriously,the pain was like labor all over again. Tears started flowing,but I enjoyed what I was experiencing at the moment. He was cumming inside of me and I felt it. I wanted to keep fucking while he was cumming, so I put both legs around his neck. He slowly fucked me while he was still cumming and he started playing with my pussy.

His dick was still hard, I got up off his dick and cleaned myself up and listened to him bitch:

"You better not be fucking nobody else! I'm not whipped or nothing, but I asked you when we started this was *the pussy always gone be this good*. I didn't believe you honestly, and it's not just your pussy it's everything. I really will beat yo' ass if I find out you giving *my* pussy away. Oh, and I'ma beat the nigga ass too!" He was walking up on me taking shit, naked and his dick is swinging. I figured by the time he made it over my way, I would suck his dick if he would just shut up already. Instead, he continued to talk. I didn't want him sitting next to me, so I stretched out on the couch on my back and I tilted my head off the couch and said, "Come put your dick in my mouth and shut the fuck up, got damn!" He just stood there, so I grabbed him by his balls and walked him closer to my mouth and sucked his dick. I had him sliding all around in a circle; he couldn't hold his balance, plus he had on socks – all the while, on the wooden floors.

I said, "Grab the couch and stop all that running like a bitch." He got upset and rammed his dick in my throat, but as he exited my throat, I caught on to the tip and bit him. I had a cup of ice on the table but it was ice water mixed with minimal ice by the time I touched it again. I pulled his dick out and told him I was done, and I'm sitting there getting a drink of water. Suddenly, he pulls me by the legs. The icy water runs behind my neck and ears and I was low-key pissed, but he started sucking my toes. He turned me over and licked the water off me which was down my spine at this point.

Of course, he didn't stop there; he started kissing my ass and I took it upon myself to start clapping my ass on his face. Spreading my ass apart, he stuck it in, tongue deep in my ass – I started fucking his tongue. It felt great, but I wanted to be spanked. I stood up and bent over and he hit me with all force ten times. The pain could've ended sooner,but I tuned him out so he spanked me again and again until his hand started burning. I don't care the amount of pain, I'm not going to say 'stop' or give in. He stopped and I sat on his lap and he said, "I will give you anything you want. Just don't play with me, don't fuck nobody else. I would never give another woman what I'm giving you now, and what I'm trying to give you in the future."

He was just too friendly and I didn't want to hear that shit, so I faced the wall silently. Next thing I know, this motherfucka' turned off the TV and lamp and went in the bedroom. Sitting in the dark, I burst out laughing and I lay there naked for a minute. Then, I got up and went to the bedroom he was in,and stood in the doorway. The whole house is midnight blue, and my shadow is visible [like human form – it was almost scary]. "What?" He asked. I replied, "Can I come lay next to you?" He turned over and faced the wall. I walked around to my side of the bed and got under the cover, and this motherfucka' turned and faced me. He said, "Come here man."I laid my head on his chest and felt his dick getting hard, so I'm rubbing his dick with my leg and when my legs opened,he stuck his arm between them. We laid there just holding one another and I tried to doze off,but I felt him nudging me. I did not move because if he knew I was 'up-up,' it would be some more fucking. He whined: "Babbbyyy… come here!" I didn't respond. "Lissa, you ain't sleep,so stop playing. I told you stop getting my dick hard and going to sleep."My giggling ass just had to laugh. I replied, "Come on baby, fuck me."

He was fucking me on and off the bed. He was fucking the life out of me, and putting life in me all at the same damn time. He said, "Get on this dick, you already know I need you to ride this dick." I rolled over because I didn't want his dick out of me, and I got on top – it was a bull ride from under! This man was fucking me saying, "You always wanna fuck and fuck. Look at you, a nigga giving you what you want, and you slumped over… bitch get up!" Choking him, I tell him to 'shut the fuck up' and I sit on his dick real proper-like. I accepted his challenge, and I started fucking him hard to where when we touch, we're smacking. He looked at me like: 'slow down,' but I jumped harder and harder. I looked him in his eyes and said, "Fuck yo pussy!"

He grabbed me by my hair and said, 'stop.' I reached behind me and rubbed his balls and said, "Bust wherever you'd like." He choked me with both hands and fucked me as hard as I was fucking him. I could barely breathe, but I managed to whisper: "Nut in this pussy,it's your pussy." He fucked me even harder to the point where I was jumping off his dick and landing back on it. I had an orgasm in mid-air and landed back on his dick in the middle of said orgasm,and started cumming and gushing while screaming. I was trying to ride it all out; he is cumming while watching me go insane and all of the sudden, the bed dropped! Not giving a fuck about the bed,we went to the bathroom and cleaned each other up and went to bed. We fucked until 4 in the morning off and on.

7:43AM, my phone is going off and I'm pissed. I tell him to answer the phone and it's motherfuckas on the other end arguing. I tell him to turn it off and I'll handle it later. His phone starts going off. Now I'm extra pissed – sex don't mean shit the night before,if you can't enjoy the morning after. I'm up with an attitude. I get up and make the bed, feeling drunk and dizzy looking for my clothes.

Irritated like a motherfucka, I'm ignoring this man while he's talking. He's saying why I shouldn't have an attitude and I could really just stay in the bed all day. I scream for him to shut up because here it is 8 o'clock and he was on my nerves! He came and kissed me. I told him goodbye and went to walk out the door. He called my name. I looked back and he looked me in my eyes and told me he loved me. I rolled my eyes and slammed the door.

Processing everything he had just said, I'm sitting in the car like, "Lissa, you didn't even have to do all that – plus he said 'I love you,' girl." (first time he said it and wasn't drunk). I started the car, and I walked back in the house. He started laughing: "Yeah, calm yo' ass down. Did you come in here to apologize?" I told him 'hell no,' I just wanted to kiss his lips again, and tell him I loved him back. Leaving out the door with less attitude, I went home and got some more rest.

Later that night,we went to the bar since I flaked the night before and man… did I get drunk! Soon as we got to the bar,he pissed me off like he always does. I ended up cursing him out, and I walked in alone. I ordered me a shot of scotch, and three men offered to pay for it; that put me in an even angrier mood. It was packed with niggas and wanna-be fly bitches. (the grandmothers that don't think they raisins yet) I sat far off and he came in and stood where I was sitting. Somebody must have been looking my way,because this fool tells me to come sit by him,just for him to stand in front of me. He handed me some dollars, I put it in the jukebox and right then, the drink hit me. I wanted to fuck, so I sat my ass down because one more shot, and we would have been all over each other.

I'm sitting there and this high yellow bitch is at the bar with her nigga and she's dancing on him. She gets their drinks and he went his way and she stayed at the bar. Again, I'm sitting behind this man so nobody can really see me. She kept dropping her phone and bending over. Then, this bitch looked up like the camera man said: "get ready for the close up of your cumshot." She started walking towards my dude all sexy and shit, and right when she was close enough to side hug him, I came from behind him and fucked him down while she just stood there. He started laughing and said, "You crazy, baby. You saw that bitch coming this way, huh?" I said, "She ain't stupid… and neither are you. We won't go there cause three niggas in here offered to buy that drink you got your lips on right now."

He replied, "She ain't fucking with you, baby… and which niggas?" I laughed and kept dancing until my song went off and he was like: "When you start dancing like that? Fuck this, let's go… I'm ready for that pussy!" We got to the house and we didn't waste any time. He carried me to the bed and kissed me all over. He fucked me rough. Sex didn't last that long that night. He was still on a power-trip from the night before – he really just wanted to sleep inside of me. Skin to skin, blackened by the dark, I listened to him breathe and I ran my fingertips all over his body.

He flipped the light on and said, "Baby let's fix the bed." (The slats were broken and the bed came apart) I slapped the wall down trying to get that light off. "It's three in the morning… unless we fucking,go to bed, damn," I said jokingly – I was dead ass serious. He said, "Naw baby, the bed is down and you wore me out. We can't keep fucking like this." I said, "Well let's go fuck on the porch one time for the one time!" He started raising his voice: "You need to go back to counseling!"

Stack

I walked in '*The Stack*' solo as usual, just to grab a drink and go. I peeped the scene when I opened the door, and I sat there quietly. There were 15 people total including the owner and bartender. This man's game [of pool] had just finished, and he came and had a seat next to me. I didn't know this man. I've noticed him in *The Stack* before, but I hang with niggas, so people never know if it's okay to speak.

There were two ladies (*we'll call them 'T' and 'Friend'*) sitting at the bar, trying to draw his attention. 'T' called me over there and when I walked up, they both said, "Damn!" (I laughed because I already knew) 'T' said, "*You smell like a whole pound.*" 'Friend' followed up and said, "*You should have let me hit it.*"

He [the man that was playing pool] was drunk, but alert, and was funny as hell. He asked me what was I drinking….(*I'm sorry I'm just not that bitch that sits at the bar waiting or wanting a man to buy her a drink.*) I told him, "I got it…." and he looked up at me, as if to say: "Lady just tell me." The bartender and I were regulars, she poured up a double shot of scotch and placed it in front of me as I'm telling him how I wouldn't let him buy me a drink. The man hurried and shoved his money for my drink in her hand and she said, "Well I'm going to take his money." He looked at me and said, "I got this, I don't mind buying you nothing." He asked for my name and he introduced himself, and during his ending sentence, he exclaimed, "You're my new friend." I was cool with that, but apparently, the other ladies were a little uncomfortable. He began asking me questions; I don't really remember what he asked first because I wasn't looking for conversation, and 'T' and I had starting talking about my book.

'T' wanted to know when another chapter was being birthed. I told her I wasn't ready to give Wichita all of me like that. The man that bought me the drink (*Let's call him 'Pool' for now*) overheard us and asked, "You're writing a book... about what?" I replied, "Just some erotica stories. Real-life based." He looked at me and said, "Tell me more." It was so funny because he was fucked up, and we were talking in each other's face. I begin to explain to 'Pool' how I was afraid to just put myself out there like that, because people only supported my stories for the simple fact that they never really knew me, and it was free business with extra details… but all real nothing less.

'Friend's loud-mouth ass blurted out, "Yeah, you talk about everybody, so a motherfucker going to pick at you and talk about you as well." I looked down there at the bitch (*because not only was I not talking to you… but bitch, you've never read a story*.) As I'm looking coldly at this funky bitch, I inform her: "I'm not worried about me… I'm out here trying to protect my kids' heart, ears and eyes from the shit." 'Pool' exclaimed, "See look right there: Wichita has a dark cloud over it, nobody wants you to make it. Your stories have been shared in Wichita, nowhere else, so pull your stories and publish your book."

We finally locked eyes and it was magic – I don't know how I was able to take my eyes off this man. We talked for two hours….I usually would have got my drink to-go, but I couldn't move. I was blown away by the conversation (*I haven't had an intelligent conversation in years, and it was beautiful*). During the two hours, I read him and guessed his accurate age. I also learned his sign, a piece of his life, about his ex-wife, mother and kids. The other ladies were just dying to be a part of our conversation, so he ordered them another drink…. just to shut them up. He got up to talk to a man [his cousin], who raped me (*with his eyes*). 'T' couldn't wait to come sit next to me, telling me about how '*in her drunken days*,' she put her hand down his pants, and his dick was little.

'Friend' went outside to smoke a cigarette with 'Pool'. He came back in and asked if I was hungry (*'Friend' was in the background saying, "remember when we use to go out to eat? Can you buy me breakfast? Etc.*) All he had was his cards and no cash so he couldn't drink no more. I told him to get what he wanted and I would pay for it. He looked at me like: "*really,*" and I asked him, "What?" He wanted it, and I paid for it. He said, "I'm worth more than the change I came in here with." I said, "That's your business, that has nothing to do with me." He asked me what would I do if he pulled out a stack of money. I replied, "Honestly, I would get the fuck up and walk away from you; I don't like attention, and money is one thing that I could care less about. I've fucked up money I will probably never see at one time again." By this time my phone was going off but it wasn't shit but them nasty bitches that be in my inbox on Facebook. He must have seen the girl pictures, because he asked if I was bisexual or if I had a man. (*Like damn, I can't just be single?)* I told him, "I didn't consider myself to be anything, I'm just me... hell, I get bored easily. I don't eat pussy, though. I don't like the way it tastes. I'm sorry, I just don't." He replied, "Well, have you ever tasted yourself?"

"Yes, I've tasted myself plenty of times, and I love the way I smell and taste. I might consider eating pussy – if a female tasted like me or better... I said 'might,' because I be super wet' and I'm not licking and/or sucking juices. Sometimes, I get so wet, I get embarrassed just because that's one of the things I wouldn't do, " I told him. He started rocking in the seat looking for words, but I could already read his mind. He said, *"Hmmm.... "* kind of like how T.I. would say. In his (T.I.) voice, he said, "Well, I've been craving a taste of something really good and sweet like you've described." I shook my head because no matter what I say or what I write, I ain't never been that easy.

Head doesn't really excite me, unless you can fuck off the charts. My eyes roam; one because these motherfuckers are big, and two, there's always a bitch somewhere mumbling under her funky ass breath. I wanted to see his dick, and I didn't need him to show me personally (*X-ray vision, baby)*. I just kept looking at the middle of his shorts. At any point, he could have stopped me and said, "Eyes up here," and I would have just been like: "Yeah, you're right." But he actually sat back so I could really look at it. In that moment, or a few seconds before in my head, I had already sat on his face [and I don't do that often]. In that same moment, in his head, I had fed him, burped him and fed him again.

I licked my lips, and he stared at me like he wanted to kiss me. He sighed and then grew quiet. We talked a little while longer... we talked so long, that a random man waited on us to end our conversation. He said, "It looked like you and your wife were getting deep, and I didn't want to interrupt."

He looked at me and said, "See... give me a chance to know you." I got up and walked away. I got in the car and I won't lie, I was waiting on the car to warm up (*which 1 hadn't done in forever*), but I was actually waiting on him. I'm 28, there's no need in pretending like I don't know what I need and want in my life. We connected on a level I believe I may never connect with another human. He came over to the car like I knew he would, he looked at me and said, "If I had you, I wouldn't even... cheat I'd stay put. I was hoping you didn't drive off without giving me your number. You walked off and I had to catch you. I'm going to let you know, we've got these hoes feeling some type of way already."

He said, "Your friend was tryna down you." I laughed because I have no friends in the free world. I said, "I really don't give a fuck, because no matter what was said - it wasn't said to me, so she got it. But friend, you said you were going to read my book....so to answer your question, hell yeah this is what he like." He gave me his number and told me to call his phone before I drove off. We said our 'good-byes' and he told me to text him when I got home. I texted him when I got home and he texted me. Both of us were acting like junior high kids, with a crush we couldn't control. This man stimulated my mind and melted my body with his words. I'm not talking sweet nothings; like he's so smart, open minded, has a beautiful mind and a kind soul and spirit.

I was so turned on, I started having visions of fucking him. I'm well alert of what we're saying to one another but I stripped for him, showing him my skin. He's already made love to my mind. My brain already started to block other niggas. He said, "Come to me," and I did his favorite dance while stripping down to my bra and panties. I'm already a few inches from the ground, so I crawled to him slowly and slithered up his body while he sat on the edge of the bed and watched me. I turned around, faced him and sat on his lap not caring what he would think because we just met. I put his dick inside of me and he kissed me because he wasn't comfortable moaning. The first push is everything to me, and I enjoyed him opening me up, so I moaned for the both of us. He fucked me slow and I fucked him hard. I put my feet behind him, and he laid me down halfway off the bed, and put my feet on his chest and fucked me like we'd been arguing over the kids and bills.

He said, "Baby, you get some rest and I'll get some rest." I did not want to hang up but I looked at the phone, and it was 5:31AM. We said 'goodnight' and he texted me: "I'm glad you came out tonight." I was thinking the same thing, hoping I wasn't getting ahead of myself. The next day, we texted and I felt bad that I kept him up all night. He didn't mind because he was so intrigued that he wanted to talk all day, anyways. I assured him that he had my attention and to get some rest and to call me when he got up. He called me around the time I was picking up my kids, so I didn't answer. I got my kids settled and I called him back – I love the sound of his voice over the phone.

We picked up where we left off the night before. In the middle of the conversation, he told me how he hasn't talked like we did in years and really, I knew he was telling the truth – that's how connected we were. All ears and minds open - the body wanted to follow (I mean come marching in like when the saints did). We talked marriage, additional kids, dreams, goals, marriage and kids (*because it's really a 'no' for me*). He told me he met my play mama-daughter the other day and I swear, the day me and her met for drinks, she mentioned someone by that name [I just didn't think anything of it]. She told me he was older, and when he ['Pool'] brought her up, I was just like, "fuck that and fuck him," because I had just cussed her and her mama out behind my blood sister – *I WILL NEVER FALL OUT WITH A BITCH BEHIND A NIGGA. I WOULDN'T DO IT IF I WAS MARRIED, I JUST WOULDN'T.*

I still love her, so I wouldn't do no fuck shit like that, we've been through too much together. I got quiet and I told him that she was my sister and my best friend. This nigga says, "I figured you knew her because ya'll played the same country song and ya'll kind of shaped the same." Okay, now you just want to be funny, because we're not blood... and I've got more weight on me. He got a business call, and I couldn't be more grateful because I didn't wanna talk anymore. He told me to text him and he would call me back when he was done handling business.

I sat there and you know, you can think yourself into driving your car through a motherfucker living room... Anyways, I shot him this long text about not wanting to talk anymore and some more shit. He called me and (*being the bitch I am*) of course, I didn't answer it. He sent me a long text and he was pissed; basically, he was like now I'm going to look for trouble and why do people got my name in their mouth (*really ya'll, I could've been so wrong and got him mixed up, but I didn't want to take any chances*). He texted me again and was like: "are you serious right now?" I had a session and I was proud of myself, so I went to the bar and shot him a text to let him know I didn't know if he was still out, but I was going to the bar [not on no stalker shit]. I told him that when I got there, I wouldn't speak and I would not feel any type of way if a bitch was all in his face. He texted me back and said 'stop.'

I pulled up to the stack and I finished smoking my blunt. I walked and waited on the bartender. Meanwhile, 'Pool' got up and walked over to me and said, "Really, you're gonna come in here and not speak to me?" I started laughing and I told him: "Shit... I don't interrupt what people have got going on, and I ain't no stalker – don't need you thinking that." He said, "Stop," he called the bartender and said, "get me a shot of Chivas! (they don't have *Johnny Walker Black Label*)" I was so shocked because he remembered my drink. He looked at me, smiled and said, "You know I will always buy your first drink." The bartender poured the shot and said, "That's some real shit, you're bold to drink that scotch straight like that." 'Pool' looked at me and said, "That's not for me, it's for this beautiful young lady." The whole stack looked and for a minute. I let the drink sit there, and the looks from most of the people [women] was: "damn, this bitch never say nothing to nobody," but one look was from a bitch that was begging for dick from a previous sex partner that gave me a ring. 'Ooooo Weee!' That bitch couldn't wait to tell it.

Another night at the bar, we talked all night and motherfuckers wanted in on what was so funny, and why we were looking in each other's phones. He called me when he left the bar and we talked so long, we both dozed off. He woke and he texted me 'good morning.' He apologized for falling asleep and said, "Babe, I want to go see that '*Us*' movie." I shot him a text back with the movie times from both theaters and he picked the 12 o'clock showing. We were pretty bold; this was day three and we had already been around each other every day, and when we were seen out, people thought we had been together for years. We were just open – no lies, because we're not even fucking... I really want dude to be my manager. I go pick him up and I won't give up the location. But, when I pulled up, I was like: "oooookkkkkkaaaayyyy!" (We [my family] used to live in that neighborhood for some years.)

I got lost (high of course), I called him and he directed me there over the phone and when I pulled up, I froze up.... why? Nervous, of course. He walked out the house and said, "You're so shy." I just smiled because it was so true, but so was he - but he hid that shit with aggression, I liked that. Oh, [side-note] I was late but, we still made it in time and when we got there, we were in the concession stand line. The worker said, "Oh you're in the wrong line if you need tickets. I'm going to need you to go to the end." I'm thinking: *"yeah she hates her job, but Lissa don't show yo' ass in front of this man... cause bitch, 1 will yank you by that ugly ass tie."* We moved two rows over to get the tickets and then we were asked if we needed popcorn or anything else. I didn't want anything but he's like, "What's a movie without popcorn, and something to wash that dry shit down? Yeah, let me get –" but she cut him off and she said, "Oh I'm sorry sir, you'll have to go down to the concession area to get popcorn... I just sell tickets." In my head, I'm thinking: *"hmm, strike two,"* and we move back to where we were when we first walked in.

We were talking about aliens, the government and being woke... just waiting, and [of course] the same bitch that sold the tickets came. She said, "Hello, how may I help you today?" I looked at her and said sharply, "Really bitch!?" He looked at me and started laughing. I'm looking at him like: *"did this really just happen?"* It was funny as fuck, but ignorant all at the same time - that it pissed me off, too. So, we walk into the movies, there were a few people in the movies, but it wasn't packed at all. We picked a row that was up above, and it was only one person on the end. I haven't been to the movies since '*Coco*' came out, and that was with my sister and all the kids. We talked during the previews and made plans to see '*Ma.*' The movie started, and he reached over and touched my arm. I looked at him and he said, "Kiss me." I kissed him and quickly pulled back because not only do I not kiss people I haven't known for years, but he kissed me better than all them! I looked back at the screen and I couldn't help but think: *what his mouth would feel like on my private parts*. He reached for my hand this time, and we held hands and I sat our hands in my lap. He unlocked his hand and placed it on my thigh.

Low-key he was pressing my buttons – and it wasn't because he touched me, it was the way he touched me. I was with a nigga for five years and I can honestly say: *he never touched me like that*. I flinched a little, not knowing how my body would react to a stranger. We looked up at each other and his lips said: *"come here,"* and I licked his lips and we kissed like the 13-year-olds do when their parent drop them off at the mall. I had the seat warmer on, but his kisses are what melted me. He laid back in his seat and he rubbed my thighs and I had my legs crossed, but he started playing with my pussy. He was forcing his fingers into tight spots. I let him touch me, I became moist and he stopped. I looked at him because I wanted him to keep going. I wanted to grab his dick, but I don't like to be teased unless we're fucking (*don't do that to me*). I knew better than to go watch that movie with him, I was a little spooked. For one, the movie is what America needs to see, and two, I jumped and grabbed his arm (I rubbed it after because I stuck my nails in him). He tapped on my thigh and I knew what he meant, he wanted me to open my legs - I had on tights, so he could really feel my pussy.

He looked at me, pressed into my pussy and rubbed up and down. Ignoring the people in front of us (and the man at the end of the row) I started moaning. He played with my pussy faster and I moaned louder I noticed the man on the end looking but I couldn't tell him to stop I wanted him to go inside my clothes when I noticed I could hear myself over the movie I threw his hand in his lap. We both laughed, then we kissed and really watched the movie. After the movie was over, we got up to leave and when I stood up, I noticed there were seven people sitting behind us. I never said anything, I just got up and walked with the small crowd. We talked every day, but his occupation prohibited us from really just spending time together – plus we needed to slow down, I thought.

Two nights later, a lady (Lala) I see for sex topics was like, "I've never really met you, come out and drink tonight." I replied, "I'll be out by 11:00PM, let me finish typing a story and editing a video." Lala sent me a text that said: "*bet*." I was there by 11:45PM, but I finished my blunt. I walked in at midnight. She said surprised, "Finally!" I just laughed and the bartender poured my shot. (*It's just fucking sad at this point that she knows to just pour me up one when I sat down*). I had one shot and she was like, "Damn do they take cards?" I told her, "No girl, just cash," and she was like, "Damn do you want to run to the ATM with me?" I replied, "Come on, they've got an ATM in *711* in the Lynwood area." We get to the store and 'Pool' text me and was like: "*what you doing?*" I told him I was at the *Haystack*, but I ran to the ATM and would be back. He didn't text me back and I got back to *The Stack* five minutes after I sent that text. I was laughing at something Lala had said as I entered the building… I opened the door and there he was. I was surprised but excited to see him!

We just looked at each other. I finally sat down and told the bartender to get me another shot. 'Pool' came to my end of the bar faster than *The Flash*. Lala was like, "Damn he came down here quick." It caused a little scene, but we didn't mind. He just looked at me and told me he missed me and walked off. I missed him too and as he walked away, I was just like: *how did this even become us?* I got up to leave and I walked over to him to let him know, and he got up to walk me out. He pushed the door open and held it as I walked through, and as soon as we stepped on the porch, I kissed him. His kisses are everything – I didn't even *need* to fuck him. He put his hand in the middle of my back and grabbed me. We kissed deeper and I was moaning and he said, "You missed me too, huh?" I smiled and told him that I missed his face. I asked him why he didn't tell me he was out tonight (only because I would've chilled with him, instead of coming to the bar to meet Lala).

He said, "Honestly, I didn't want to come here (*The Stack*) – *I hate it here*. My cousin wanted to come have a drink. I saw your car and I was like: *that's baby car,* so I didn't mind after that....

when I came inside, I didn't see you. You parked ducked off this time, so I didn't know what to think." I told myself: *'we're about to have our first little-ole argument.'* I'm laughing because when I flipped out on him he said, "Nah, I thought you said it wasn't going to be any of that…" so I shot that shit right back at him, because I haven't even fed him my pussy yet. We're' goofy as fuck, so we laughed that shit off and his cousin and Lala walked out the bar. His cousin was like, "She's bad, grab her ass." I told him to 'shut up' and 'Pool' was like: *"that nigga crazy,"* but he grabbed my ass anyway, and I pushed him in the chest. "So you're gonna do it?" I asked He said, "You knew I was going to do that anyways," and he kissed me and hugged me 'goodbye,' telling me was going to be out a couple more hours, and then he would go home. I asked him what he had to do that was going to keep him out late and he replied, "I gotta handle somethings baby," and I told him to be safe and to text or call me when he made it home.

Lala was still in the parking lot (*she stays up the street from me),* so I asked her if she wanted to match – she's always down for whatever. I went home and changed into something comfortable and went to her house. We were talking about random shit, and I was telling her about my first radio call and how annoyed I was with the one pervert that wouldn't chill. I also ran a few topics by her for the next show. I was on FaceBook and saw where a girl said she liked extra spit when she's fucking, and another female said she wants to experience an orgasm by getting fucked. Easy debates. I don't like spit at all; it's a turn off – and you don't even want to know *those consequences for a move like that.* I demand an orgasm every time I fuck, or I will never look your way again! We were so deep in the conversation, I didn't answer the first time *Mr. Pool* called [*He received 'Mr.' because he has earned it*]. After he called, he became an easy topic, which was fine simply because there was nothing to tell anybody. She asked, "Is he waiting on you to get home?" I answered 'no.' She followed up, "Do ya'll stay together?" I looked at her crazy because months prior to that, I know she saw me in there (*The Stack*) with my ex-sex partner. I said, "He's handsome, ain't he?" She replied, "Yes, he looks good."

I said, "Thank you, but he's single... and so am I. Honestly, we just met but our connection is fire!"

"Huh?" Lala had her mouth open in awe, "Shut up, I thought you were his wife or something... I seriously thought ya'll was doing the family thing." I was getting up to leave and he called me again, so I answered the phone and wrapped up my conversation with her. As I was walking down the steps, I said 'hello' and he asked what I was doing. I informed him that I had just left Lala's house and I was headed home.

We talked until 4:3AM, he had to be on the road by 8AM. Continuing to communicate, a few days went, but we didn't press the issue to see each other. Lala text me saying: '*stack tonight, and*' I replied, "Yep... I'll see you around 11:30PM." I walked in and Mr. Pool was there. I spoke to Lala and walked over to him and rubbed him down his back. He looked back like he didn't know it was me (*like I didn't see him look at me when I walked in*). He told the bartender to get me a shot of *Chivas* and he began telling me about one of the ladies at the bar. We laughed and I gave him his space, because at the end of the day, he's single. I went and talked to Lala and we showed each other peoples' dick photos that were sent through Facebook.

I was ready to go home; I was horny and I wasn't fucking, so i wanted to be asleep. Mr. Pool got in the car with me – I know them bitches at the bar thought we left together, but I just took him to his car (*nosy bitches*). He grabbed by my neck and kissed me and I told him to 'stop,' because we were not fucking, I wasn't getting any head and I'm not gonna be up all night, not being able to sleep because I need to cum. I told him I wanted him to touch my pussy. He laughed and said, "Baby, open your legs." I damn near popped my fucking legs off just to open them. I was already flowing for him he rubbed his finger in circles on my clit, then he moved his finger up and down before sticking his finger in me. I leaned over on the steering wheel, he took his finger out and he went to lick it, I followed suit. Licking the back of his finger while he licked the front, the juices vanished. He asked, "Why didn't you tell me that pussy taste like that, you're wrong. You smell so fucking good!" He stuck his finger back in me and fingered me real hard – I grabbed his face and kissed him. He pulled his finger out and sucked my juices off. He kissed me again and he opened the door and just got out of the car…